Never let go

Until we're gone

SANDHYA K RAVI

Never let go

Until we're gone

SANDHYA K RAVI

PAPER TOWNS
PUBLISHERS

Presentation by Paper Towns India.
Web: www.papertownsindia.com

ISBN : 978-93-91228-31-6

First edition 2021

To the one, who unwrapped the writer in me. If not, this would have ended up as a mere dream.

Acknowledgement

This book is nothing less than a dream come true. I would like to extend my sincere thanks to everyone, who has supported me in this journey. Owing to which, it was feasible for me, to finally give wings to my dreams. In particular, I would like to mention:

My parents, for letting me pursue my passion, besides respecting my preferences.

God, without him, I wouldn't have been where I am today.

My husband, Dhinesh, who believed in me more than I could ever believe in myself.

My friend, Ishita Chatterjee, who lit the initial spark in me, to surge ahead with this whole thing.

My dearest friend, Shamili Shekar, who genuinely wished to see me as an author, one day.

Readers, for the love and acceptance.

Lastly, Paper Towns India, for turning my dreams into reality. Forever indebted.

A DAY TO REMEMBER

Froth and surf,
Etched in strand,
Stirs my soul,
Over and over,
Feels so serene
as tides flick my feet,
Imparting a ray of bliss,
Deep down my heart,
Feels so surreal,
With you by my side,
Snuggling closer,
As you embrace me in your arms,
We sat there; gazing at the sky,
Creating memories for lifetime,
Your touch sent me chills,
Deep down, as you tucked,

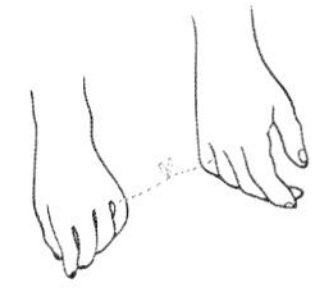

A strand of my hair,
Behind my ear,
That moment,
My heart skipped a beat,
Why does it feel
so magical?

MY SUNSHINE

You were my only hope,
Amidst the tumultuous life,
You were my only sunshine,
Amidst the never-ending darkness,
You were the only one,
Who, made my heart flutter
with utmost ecstasy.

I never really thought,
You will be the missing piece,
Of my heart's puzzle,
A void, which can never be filled,
By anyone, ever again.

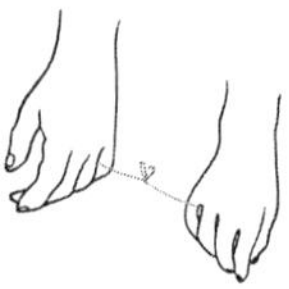

Though it feels like a dream,
It's still a good one,
Worth cherishing for yonks,
I love you,
I always will,
Until I breathe my last.

MY FEELINGS

I did shield my heart,
To quite an extreme,
I did miss you all day;
Yet never made it too obvious
or left a trace of it,
Forsaking my own feelings.

I would rather say,
I was dubious
of my own feelings,
Failing to get a grip
of what I was going through.

As time ticked,
I did ascertain,
What I had for you wasn't,

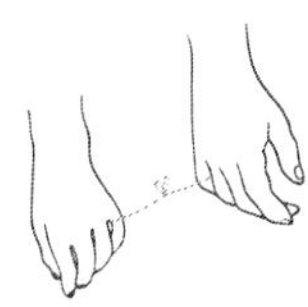

Anything lesser than love,
Since the flame would have died,
Long back if it was a mere pash.

Despite the conflicts,
I had in my mind,
The trepidation of
not ending up together,
Made me look quite closed off.

SOLITUDE

Those few moments of sheer elation,
While sipping a cup of hot coffee,
Gazing at nature's backdrop,
Nonchalant and unruffled,
Unmindful of all those clamours,
Soaked in solitude and peace,
Having a heartfelt colloquy,
With that special one,
The feeling of chill breeze,
Blowing through my face,
Seems so reviving,
Pretty much like;
icing on the cake.

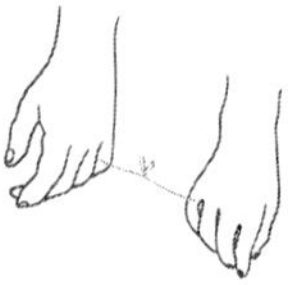

KINDNESS

Every life seems perfect,
With glitz and glam,
Everyone seems gleeful,
Like a sugar-coated candy,
Every now and then,
Just observe your true-self,
There is pain masked,
Inside everyone's smile,
There are unvoiced sufferings,
Wrapped up, in everyone's life,
Invisible yet undeniable,
Unfathomable and inexplicable,
Not everyone can cognize,
What someone is up to,
Life is not a bed of flowers,
Dive deep, every milestone,

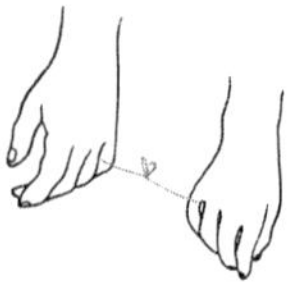

Has an untold story,
The world is unaware of,
Whatever it takes,
Be kind,
The world needs more of it.

MY WHOLE WORLD

When I first met you,
I had no clue,
You would eventually
become my whole world,
One fine day.

You would mean so much,
That the mere thought
of losing you,
Scared the wits out of me,
How did we get too close?
I still wonder.

What have you done to me?
I feel so hypnotized,
Every time our eyes locked,

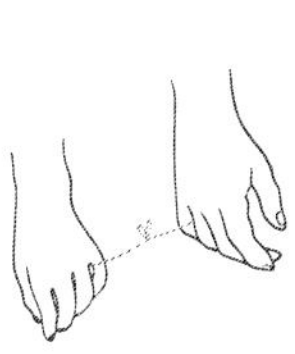

An ineffable feeling,
A dynamic pull,
Way too intense,
Feels so magical,
How deep our souls are entangled,
Inextricable by any means.

TALES OF A BROKEN HEART

Wrecked soul and broken heart,
Weary eyes; devoid of tears,
Memories haunting day and night,
Physically alive; emotionally dead,
Shattered dreams; chaotic as hell.

Stumbling upon the topsy- turvy love,
Not knowing, how to hold on,
Letting go wasn't easy,
Nevertheless, holding on,
Seemed a way too painful,
Depression engulfed her,
Bit by bit.

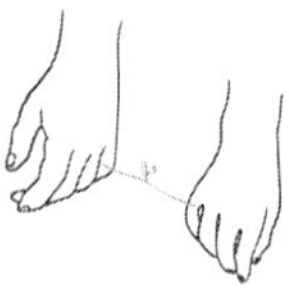

Her heart was a broken rummer;
Shattered into pieces,

Her love was a spilled wine;
Spilled all over the floor,
She was a complete mess,
Will he return to mend her soul?

ALL THAT I CRAVE FOR

Sitting in a cosy place,
Near the casement window,
Gazing at the velvety blue sky,
Earphones on,
Listening to my favourite track,
Flipping through the pages,
Of a dreamy engaging novel,
Drenched in words,
With a much needed
dose of caffeine,
Is all that I crave for,
Besides, it makes me feel euphoric,
Unveiling my inner solitude,
With some 'me time',

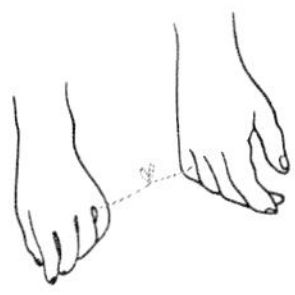

Far away from hubbub and faces,
Rediscovering the new me,
Amidst peace and bliss.

WE WEREN' T DESTINED

Unsure; why fate was so unfair,
We weren't destined,
We weren't meant
to be forever,
It's so hapless of us,
Nevertheless, what we shared
was quite real and incredible,
A feeling, so unique and intense,
A bond, so unparalleled,
Souls so entwined,
Forever and beyond,
Though physically apart,
We do connect so deep,
On an emotional level,
We crossed paths
for some reason,

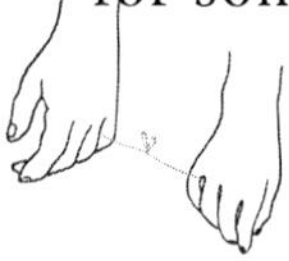

I am glad to have known you,
To have loved you,
You were the best thing
that has ever happened in my life,
Though we aren't fated,
The love is real,
'We' are real; profoundly real.

LOVE

If love was the sky;
They were the moon
and the stars,
If love was a cloud;
They were the rain
and the rainbow,
If love was the ocean;
They were the froth
and the surf,
If love was the woods;
They were the night
and the fireflies,

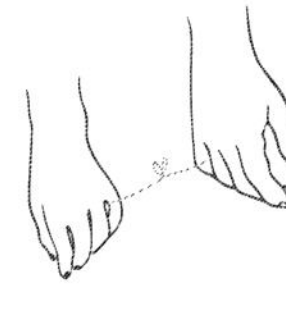

If love was travel;
They were the photographs
and the memories,
If love was everything;
They were the universe
and the Galaxies.

DOES LOVE NEED VALIDATION?

He figured out,
I was a Picasso,
When it comes
to bottling up,
My feelings for him,
Yet, he failed to decipher,
I was yearning so long,
To unwrap my heart,
To express
my deepest feelings,
Since, a long time now.

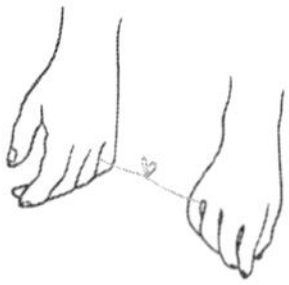

I wonder if it's too late,
Maybe, I should have,
Opened-up a little earlier,
But does love need validation?
If your hearts knew
each other, so well,
Our eyes have spoken volumes,
A language, only our hearts
are capable of decoding,
Will this not suffice?

MEMORIES

She heard the paintings,
Talking and whispering
his name,
Indeed, she was,
So smitten in love with him.

Every track;
In her playlist,
Every photo;
In her gallery,
Almost everything,
Evoked memories
about him,
Moving her to tears.

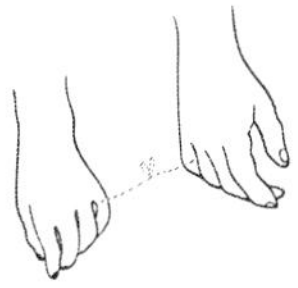

INSPIRATION

Her demeanour was,
Self-effacing and demure,
A meek wallflower,
Mediocre of all sorts,
Yet, one of a kind,
His love,
Revamped her in ways,
No one can ever imagine,
His love,
rejuvenated her soul,
Augmented her morale,
His love,
Made her unearth,
The hidden potential,
To shatter the glass ceiling
which she was confined to,

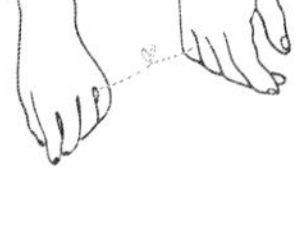

Right from her childhood,
His love,
Inspired her,
To reach heights,
She bloomed,
Like never before,
She felt as though,
She could conquer,
Everything that
came her way,
With him by her side.

WILL SHE FIND TRUE LOVE?

In a world where
dallying seemed,
The new normal and
True love was,
Few and far between,
She felt disenchanted,
Hopeless of finding,
A perfect love.

She was longing for,
Something quite stable and solid,
Something beyond physicality,
She fancied soul intimacy,
Rather than physical intimacy,
Someone who would,

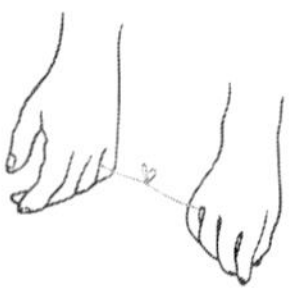

Stick around,
Through thick and thin,
Someone, whom she could
rely on without any scruples,
Someone, who felt like home.

NEVER LET DOWN

She slumped onto the floor,
Dolorous and spineless,
Being drenched completely,
As the water from shower
kept gushing ceaselessly,
Tears streamed down her face,
As the words kept echoing,
She was shattered,
Unable to apprehend,
What had transpired.

What hurt her wasn't
what was said,
But who had said,
That really did matter,
It felt quite impossible,

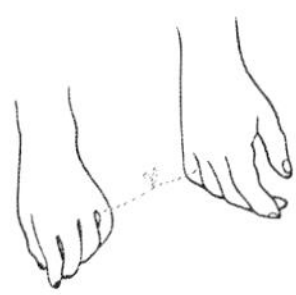

To come to terms,
But reality hit her hard,
The words he spoke,
Pierced through her heart,
Imparting an excruciating pain,
She felt as though,
Her heart was bleeding,
Not in her vivid dreams,
She thought, he would
offend her so bad;
Yet, it happened,
That's how it panned out.

CAN WE START AFRESH?

From stealing glances,
When everyone was around,
To holding hands,
When no one was around,
We did come a long way,
If I had only known,
All this would soon,
Turn into memories,
I would have restrained
from falling so deep,
In love with you,
I still do envisage,
A heartfelt conversation
with you,

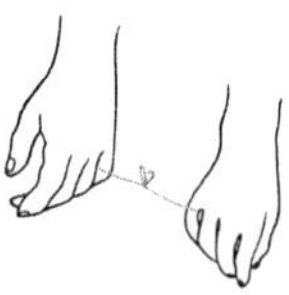

Maybe for one last time,
You do owe me,
At-least a goodbye,
It feels heavy to see you
exit my life, so abruptly,
I repudiate your excuses,
Rather, can we start afresh?
Instead of calling it quits,
I do know it's too late,
Maybe, the next lifetime?

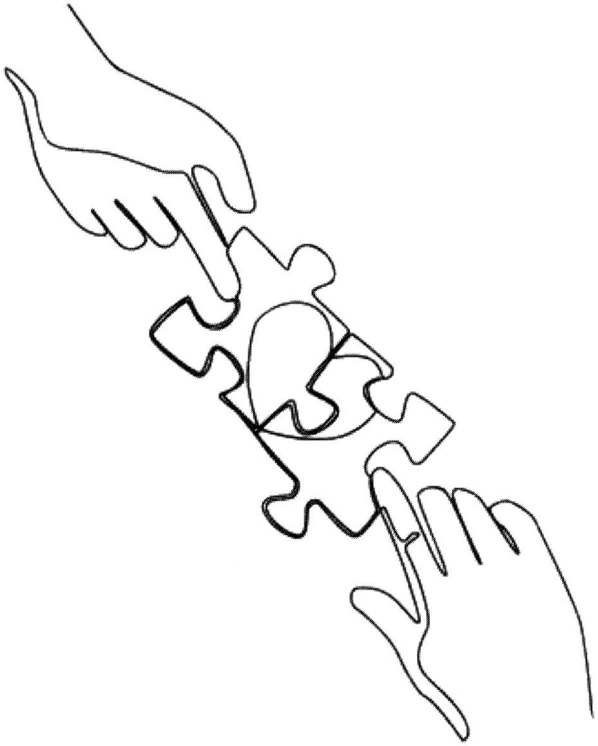

WE ARE NEVER APART

Never did I trifle,
Never did I treat you
as a mere option,
You were my priority,
Though we have parted ways,
I would keep cheering for you,
From a nook,
I would cherish
those happy times we spent,
For years to come.

All that I ever want from you,
Is to see you happy,
To see you prosper,
We are never apart, I see you in me,

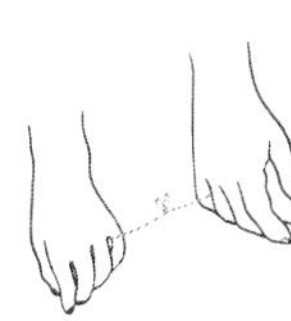

Hope I did mean
something to you,
Did I?

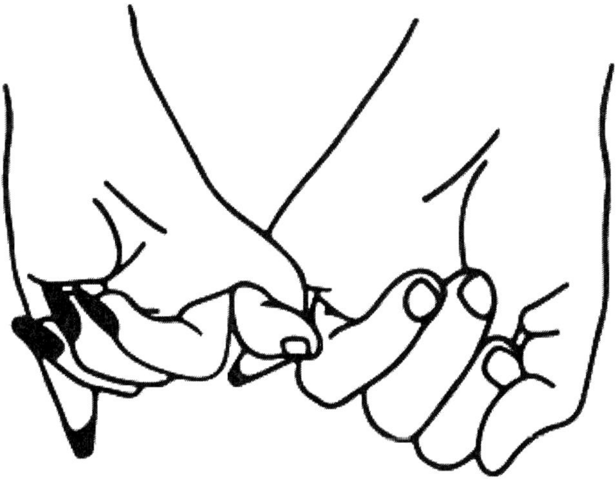

LOVE FOUND HER

She did discern,
He was significant,
She did fathom,
It was something,
Beyond friendship;
Since, her eyes,
Kept probing for him
quite often;
Yet, her heart
was too stubborn to accept,
Destiny had other plans,
She fell in love,
Exactly at that moment,
When she made up her mind,
Not to fall for him,
His charm and wit,

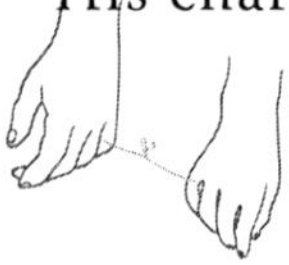

Swept her off her feet
and she gave in,
Unable to resist,
The intense feelings
which enticed her soul.

YOU LET ME DOWN

I did count on you,
Only to have my trust,
Being broken by you,
The faith I had in you,
Intrinsically blemished,
In the Fullness of time,
Ravaging my fragile heart,
Annihilating my feelings
and lacerating my soul.

You let me down.
I wasn't prepared for this,
Not in my worst dreams;
Yet, you let me down,
I wouldn't Inculpate you;

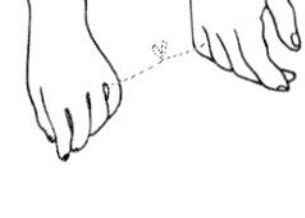

Since, it was entirely,
My fault, for having,
Trusted you blindly.

IT'S JUST THE MEMORIES WE ARE LEFT WITH!

Tears welled up,
Her eyes glistened,
Memories flashed,
As she skimmed
through the photographs,
She longed,
To go back in time,
She would have,
If it was viable,
But all she could do,
Was to gaze ardently,
Harking back to moments,
Once treasured,
Which would remain intact,

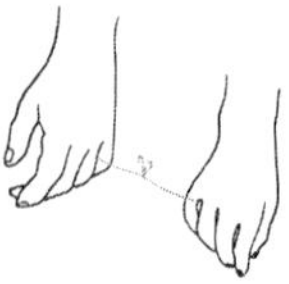

Sealed in heart,
Forever and ever,
Until her last breath.

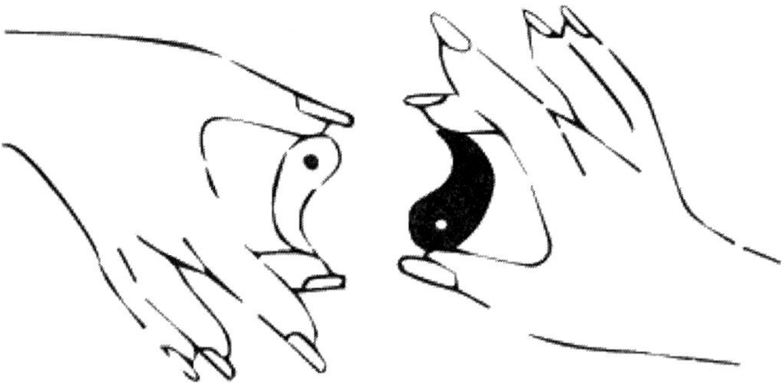

SHE IS, 'YOU'

Her heart; so fragile,
Her soul; so wondrous,
Her love; so profound,
Her vibe; so dynamic,
Her dreams; so astounding,
Her aura; so splendid,
Her humour; so witty,
Her features; so well etched.

She was a woman of substance,
She was a twilight;
Shimmering so bright
in the evening sky,
She was the silver lining

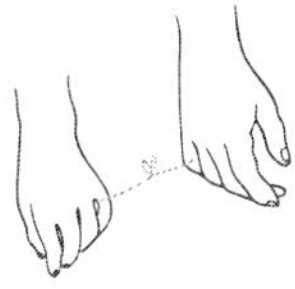

of the vibrant rainbow,
She was someone,
Simple and elegant;
Yet, one in a million.

THOUGHTS

My thoughts,
Kept orbiting around you,
Like the earth revolves
around the sun,
Least did I know,
You were eventually,
Turning out to be my obsession,
It's more of a task,
To keep you off my thoughts;
Since, you are embedded,
So deep in my heart,
I do try to keep it low-key,

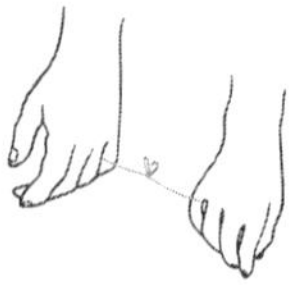

Acting all cool,
Yet, you do catch me off-guard,
Every now and then.

THE TRUTH

Sometimes, I do feel insubstantial,
Feeling completely drained,
Unable to surge ahead;
Since, the past keeps,
Haunting me day and night.

None can decipher,
The pain, I have been through;
Since the day, voidness
inhabited my heart,
For, I have never let anyone,
See my scars.

No longer, I feel responsible,
For the way, others judge me

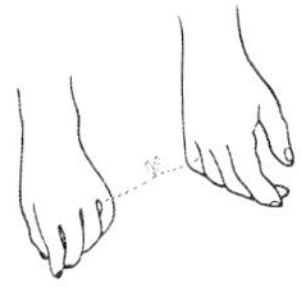

and perceive me,

For, I am deadbeat,
Constantly torn between other's
opinions,
And my own life choices.

Unless, I am true to my-self,
Unless, my smile doesn't dull
other's shine,
Unless I ain't the reason,
Behind someone's pain,
I, no longer feel accountable,
For, I am Loyal to whom I am
and to everyone, I have known.

NEVER LET GO, UNTIL WE'RE GONE!

'Forever' may seem
too expensive for,
Destiny to afford;
Still, never let go,
Until memories fade,
Until the world ceases,
Until the radiant Sun
loses its shimmering spark,
Until the waning moon
loses its gleaming gloss,
Until the zillion stars
loses its sparkle,
Until birds stop chirping,

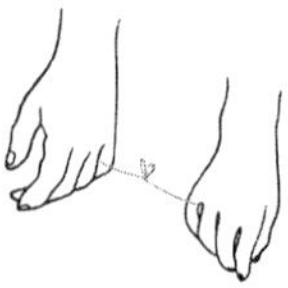

Until heavens collide
and the universe dwindles,
Never let go,
Until we are gone.

TRANQUILITY

Faint shades of white,
Silhouette of sunshine,
Empty coffee mugs,
Melancholic music filling
the secluded space,
Leaving trails of silence,
In between hazy tones,
Copiously aesthetic way,
Of spending time together,
Sequestered from babel.

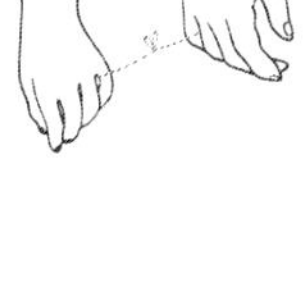

LIFE'S CHAOS

Sometimes she froze out,
Seemed reticent,
Since she knew,
It's quite intricate,
To end up together,
Considering the chaos,
She was dealing in life,
She seemed detached,
Owing to the fear of
getting heart broken,
For her heart was so delicate,
As fragile as a glass.

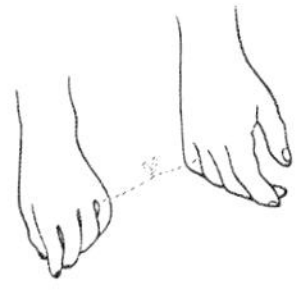

LOVE SO UNIQUE

Gaze so deep,
Smile so mischievous,
Being high on humour,
Few things left unsaid,
Enveloped inside heartstrings,
Few moments cherished,
Well etched in heart space,
Short-lived, yet saccharinc,
One in a million kind of love.

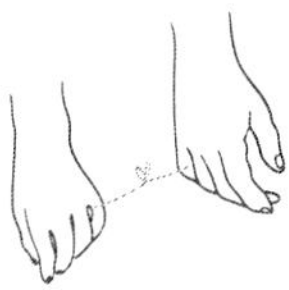